Magical Moon Cat

Jax daringly reached out with the tip of her finger and touched the little alien cat. Its fur was the softest thing she'd ever felt, softer even than Mum's precious cashmere sweater.

It seemed to Jax that she had waited for this moment her whole life. "I knew I'd find you one day!" she whispered. "Did you know you'd find me?"

Magical Moon Cat

Moonbeans
and the Dream Café

Annie Dalton

USBORNE

For Miss Bartholomew and the girls of LIIK,
St Catherine's, Bramley

First published in 2012 by Usborne Publishing Ltd., Usborne House, 83-85 Saffron Hill, London ECIN 8RT, England. www.usborne.com

Text copyright © Annie Dalton, 2012 Cover illustration by Tuesday Mourning. Inside illustrations by Katie Lovell. Illustration copyright © Usborne Publishing Ltd, 2012

The right of Annie Dalton to be identified as the author of this work has been asserted by her in accordance with the Copyright, Designs and Patents Act, 1988.

The name Usborne and the devices are Trade Marks of Usborne Publishing Ltd.

A CIP catalogue record for this book is available from the British Library.

ISBN 9781409526315

JFMAM JASOND/12 02592/1

Printed in Dongguan, Guangdong, China.

Contents

Pink lightning in Goose Green

1

Jax stood on a wobbly chair, sticking up glow-stars on the only part of the ceiling she could reach, the sloping part just above her bed.

She was wearing woollen leggings tucked into a pair of woolly socks, and a knitted beanie pulled right down over her ears. It was supposed to be April, but the cold wind whistling through the cracked window frame made it feel like the middle of winter.

Jax had had hundreds of glow-stars where they lived before. Mum had found a star chart

of Dad's and they'd spent hours arranging the stars into proper constellations. This time Mum had only bought two measly packs. Jax was going to run out of stars any minute, but she went on stubbornly sticking and sticking, because she didn't know what else to do.

Jax's full name was Ellie Mae Jackson, but everyone called her Jax; everyone except her mum, and Jax was still working on her. Jax was determined to be a world-famous scientist when she grew up, and you didn't hear of too many scientists called Ellie Mae.

A week ago today, Jax's mum had brought her to live over a shabby little café in a rundown area called Goose Green. Mum wanted to turn it into a welcoming family place where people could bring their kids and chat to their friends after they'd done their shopping. "It was such a bargain, I *had* to buy it!" Mum told everyone.

Once, long ago, Goose Green probably had real geese, a pond, and a village green, but times had changed. Jax had seen *three* trees since she got here and none of them seemed like happy trees.

"We didn't move for the trees," Mum said when Jax pointed this out. "We moved so we could have a better life."

"I liked our *old* life," Jax had muttered under her breath.

In fact, Dolly's Diner (even its name was depressing, Jax thought) was turning out to be not such a bargain after all. The builder had charged Mum a fortune for putting in stylish new windows, then left brick dust and rubble everywhere. The boiler had broken down the

day they moved in. Mice were running around in the storeroom. There were a ton of things to put right before Mum could open for business.

That's why Jax was upstairs sorting out her room by herself. She'd been up here for hours – hanging up her clothes, deciding where to put Brad's fish tank, sticking up her favourite space posters – but this big draughty room still didn't feel like hers. Jax was crossing her fingers that her new glow-stars would do the trick.

The chair gave a dangerous wobble as Jax stretched up to stick the last, highest glow-star. She jumped down to inspect her handiwork and almost cried.

The stars just looked like silly bits of stuck-on plastic. Her new home was so depressing that even glow-star magic couldn't work.

Jax knew you didn't get to be a famous scientist by bursting into tears every time something went wrong. Swallowing hard, she scanned her room. Something was missing, something really obvious. Suddenly she knew what it was.

Jax flew out to the landing, where stacks of boxes still waited to be unpacked. She found the box she needed, dragging it into her room.

Before they moved, Mum had finally given in and let Jax have Dad's telescope. She carefully unpacked it, setting it up in front of her window.

Better, she thought, and gave the telescope a loving little stroke.

Jax still remembered

the first time her dad had let her look through it. She'd had no idea what she was supposed to be seeing, but he didn't try to rush her. Dad was always telling her she was as quick as a box of frogs, easily smart enough to figure things out by herself.

Jax smiled to herself, remembering how her dad would talk to her about stars and space, using words like *nebula…supernova…solar flares*. She didn't understand most of them, but they left fiery trails in her mind, like strange poems she longed to understand.

"A lot of scientists believe that humans are all alone in the universe," Dad told her once. "But I think aliens are probably watching us right this minute, from worlds just as extraordinary as ours."

Jax was only five then and the word "alien" made her think of scary monsters. Dad had quickly explained that "alien" was just another word for "stranger", somebody you didn't know yet.

Her dad had died in a car accident just a few days before her sixth birthday. She would always miss him, but having his telescope in her room made him feel a little less far away. He had loved stars and planets so much and now, because of Dad, Jax loved them too.

She put her eye to the telescope and gave a surprised snort. She could see right into the house opposite! A gloomy-looking boy was tapping away on his computer. He had that floppy kind of hair that made Jax want to grab a pair of scissors and help him chop his way out. A giant cuddly toy was propped up on the desk beside him – an enormous white rabbit. "Big baby, still playing with toys," she jeered under her breath, then gave a squeak of surprise as the toy rabbit went lolloping across the desk. It was real! Jax had never heard of an *indoor* rabbit.

It hadn't occurred to her to use Dad's telescope for spying on people before. Feeling oddly guilty and excited, Jax moved on to the house next door, where a girl in a pink frilly leotard was practising a super-bouncy tap-dance routine. The girl kept making mistakes, mainly

because a fluffy little dog kept getting in her way. Jax thought she should stop doing that stupid bouncy dance and take her dog out to play ball.

It's not fair. Everyone else has got a pet, she thought.

Dad used to call Jax "the cat magnet". Cats were always trotting up to her to be stroked. Unfortunately, Mum was allergic to fur. She was also allergic to feathers and about a zillion other things. She wasn't allergic to fish scales, though, which is why Jax was allowed to have Brad.

She had tried to bond with her goldfish, giving him a plastic shipwreck and a sunken treasure chest to make his tiny world more exciting. She couldn't tell if Brad was impressed. Like all goldfish, he just had 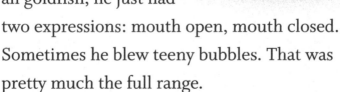 two expressions: mouth open, mouth closed. Sometimes he blew teeny bubbles. That was pretty much the full range.

Jax worried that Brad had guessed how

disappointing she found him. It would be so depressing if your actual owner thought you were boring. Just the thought made her feel like a terrible person.

She stopped spying on their neighbours and made herself go over to talk to him. "Poor fishy," she told him softly. "It's not your fault."

That's when it happened. *FLICKER-FLASH!*

Her room turned fiery pink as a ball of hot-pink light whizzed past her window, heading straight for their backyard.

Jax flew back to the window. She expected to see people rushing out into their back gardens, gazing up in fear and wonder. But Jax seemed to be the only person who had noticed. Grabbing her pocket torch, she dashed out of her room.

Welcome to Planet Earth

2

Jax hurtled down two flights of stairs. As she reached the hall, a surprise gust of wind plucked at her beanie. Like a girl astronaut in deepest space, her hair went streaming backwards. So much fresh air was whooshing around their hall that all the torn ends of wallpaper were flapping like tattered flags in a parade.

In a flash, Jax took everything in. Now they were living in the big bad city, Mum kept the back door firmly closed. Something had made it burst open – maybe the force of the blast?

Her heart thumped as she peeped out into their backyard. She was expecting burning bushes, maybe a smoking patch of ground where the lightning ball had just crashed to Earth. But the yard looked the same as usual.

It *looked* the same, but it *felt* totally different. There was a fierce fizzing in the air that made her tingle all the way up from the soles of her feet to the roots of her hair.

The busy scrubbing sounds in the café had suddenly stopped.

"Ellie?" Mum said sharply. "Did you just open the back door?"

"Yes," Jax fibbed. "I needed some air."

Jax had a private theory about what had just happened, one that she wasn't ready to share with her mum. That pink lightning...Jax didn't think it was normal lightning. It was something far more thrilling, something she'd been hoping and wishing for ever since the day her dad first told her about aliens. Today her wish had come true. An alien spaceship had landed in her backyard. The violent fizzing was just leftover cosmic energy from its long fiery journey through space.

What had happened to the ship? Maybe it had put up an invisibility shield? Or maybe, having arrived safely at its destination, it had somehow dissolved, leaving its passenger stranded on a strange planet with no way to get back home?

Jax's heart was racing now. Had an alien really landed in Goose Green? If so, how come no one else had noticed it falling to Earth? Everyone had just carried on as normal; everyone except Jax.

Jax wondered how it would feel to arrive on a strange planet all by yourself. She pictured the alien cowering in its hiding place, jumping at every sound, not daring to trust the human girl in the doorway. In movies, ignorant people sometimes handed aliens over to cold-hearted scientists for their evil experiments. The alien might think Jax was that kind of human.

"I'd never hurt you, though," she whispered. "I'm your friend."

Jax had brought her torch to hunt for traces of the burned-out lightning ball; now she had a better idea. She carefully shone the light on herself to show the alien that she was just a harmless human girl.

"Ellie! What are you thinking of, letting in this awful wind?"

Jax spun round. Mum had come up behind her without Jax hearing. There wasn't time to think up a fib, so she babbled the first thing that came into her head, which was the truth. "Mum, I saw this pink fireball hurtling out of the sky. I think it came from another world—"

Her mum quickly held up her hand. "Ellie Mae Jackson, stop right there! I've got enough on my plate. I don't need you going on about aliens."

"Mum, I *saw* it actually land in our yard!"

"No, Ellie, you didn't," Mum snapped. "Aliens do not just land in people's yards, not in real life."

Jax could feel herself going hot all over. Mum had as good as told a listening alien that it didn't exist! "But Dad said—"

"I know what your dad said, sweetie. He was fascinated by other worlds. But I have to earn my living in *this* world, and right now I have to get this café up and running, before all our money runs out."

"Dad would have believed me," Jax muttered under her breath.

Her mum took a deep breath. "There's a card from a local pizza place somewhere. Why don't you order us something to eat?"

"Okay," Jax said with a sigh. She was starving, she realized. Mum had been too busy clearing up brick dust and scrubbing walls to think about lunch.

"Order any kind you like," Mum told her. "But first shut that door, before this wind turns the café inside out!"

 Jax phoned in their order, then she sneaked back to the door and stealthily opened it again. She stood staring out into the dark, listening to the tattered flags of wallpaper rattling in the wind.

It had started to spit with rain, big cold drops. She couldn't leave the alien out in the wind and wet. Dad would have been horrified. What kind of welcome was that for a stranger from outer space?

Jax felt silly talking to someone she couldn't see, but scientists had to learn to get over that kind of thing. "I'm going in now, okay?" she whispered. "Come in when you're ready. My room is upstairs at the back."

She found the wedge of rubber they used for a doorstop and propped the door open just a crack. Mum would notice if she left it wide open.

Jax checked her watch. Five minutes before the pizza man was due and she had one more really important thing to do. She raced upstairs, hunted for a felt-tip pen and a piece of card, quickly scrawled a sign, then carefully stuck it on the outside of her door.

Welcome to Planet Earth, her sign said.

Jax drew a felt-tip arrow under her message so the alien would know it was supposed to go into her room, not Mum's.

The doorbell buzzed and Jax tore back downstairs. "Pizza's here, Mum!"

She raced into the café. This morning, she had helped Mum stack all the chairs on the tables. She lifted two down, then quickly swooshed a damp cloth over one of the tables. She found plates and cutlery and filled two glasses with tap water. Her heart was beating so wildly she was sure her mum would hear it.

Mum appeared with the pizza just as Jax finished laying the table. "You're all pink and flustered," she said, laughing.

"I've been rushing around getting everything ready," Jax said, which was true.

Jax and her mum sat munching pizza and slightly warm salad, surrounded by a forest of chairs. Jax longed to gobble hers down so she could run off to find the alien, but then Mum would know something was up.

"So how's your room looking?" her mum asked.

"Okay." Jax could feel a cold wind whistling around her ankles. She couldn't believe Mum hadn't noticed.

Mum put down her fork. "I know it's hard, Ellie, leaving your friends behind, but you'll soon make new ones."

"I can't get a new grandpa, though, can I?" The spiteful words just burst out.

Her mum's smile faded. "Your grandpa knows he can come and visit any time he wants. He only lives on the other side of the city."

"I liked it when he just lived round the corner," said Jax stubbornly. *And so did Grandpa,* she thought.

Grandpa had been furious with Mum for taking Jax away from her home and friends. "You start all these mad projects, Laura, and you never finish any of them!" he'd yelled at her. Jax felt her eyes prickle as she remembered the terrible things Mum and Grandpa had said to each other the last time they met.

Mum suddenly looked every bit as stubborn as Jax. "The trouble with your grandpa is he always thinks I'm wrong and he's right. Well, this time, Ellie, I'm the one who's right! When our café is a roaring success, he'll be eating his words."

Jax thought it was her mum who'd be eating her words. A few months ago she was getting excited about making hats; next year it would be something else. Jax felt guilty siding with her grandpa, but he was right. Mum never stuck at anything.

Jax was wearing her polite listening face as Mum chatted about paint colours (sunflower yellow and dove grey), but she'd gone back to thinking about the alien. Was it a girl or boy alien, or didn't aliens have those kinds of categories? Would they be able to talk in actual words, or would they need sign language?

Assuming it's got hands, she thought. Being an alien, it might have a few extra! Jax pictured a huge, many-armed creature squeezing through her bedroom door, and almost choked on her pizza. "Crumb!" she wheezed, as Mum banged her on the back. "Better now."

Finally the long meal was over. Mum had more cleaning to do before she could finish for the night. "Watch TV, if you like," she suggested to Jax.

Jax faked a yawn. "I think I'll go to bed. I'm really tired."

Mum followed her into the hall. "I won't always be this busy, Ellie. Not once the café is up and running."

But Jax had tuned her out, right after "busy". She had spotted a strange mark on the stairs.

It shimmered and sparkled in the electric light.

An alien footprint!

Jax thought her heart was going to jump out of her chest. "Don't work too late, Mum," she gabbled, racing upstairs.

Now she knew two things for certain:

1. An alien had really landed in Goose Green.

2. It was waiting upstairs.

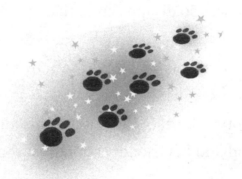

Glow-stars aren't pink!

3

"Hello!" Jax burst into her bedroom.

It was totally empty.

She was so disappointed that she felt an actual physical pain in her chest. She had been so sure that she would find the alien waiting.

Then she just felt angry. This was the telescope's fault. It had got her thinking about her dad and his friendly strangers from outer space.

Jax almost stamped her foot, because life was so unfair. Her dad was wrong. Jax *was* all alone in the universe. She was as alone as any human child in the entire history of the world; so totally alone that she had fooled herself into believing that an alien had landed in her garden.

She started to undress, sniffing back angry tears. She was going to pull her duvet over her head and pretend she'd never even *heard* of aliens.

Her teeth were chattering as she dived into her flannel PJs, leaving on her woolly socks. She was still shivering, so she added a warm cardigan and pulled her beanie back on.

She could hear loud pop music floating up from downstairs. Mum had turned on the radio to help the work go faster. Jax climbed into bed and switched off her lamp. Her room filled with a soft, flickering pink light.

That's funny. Jax hadn't realized Mum had bought *pink* glow-stars. They also gave off a really lovely smell. *It's because I've turned out the light*, she thought. Smells were always stronger in the dark.

One Christmas, when Dad was still alive, Jax had found a jelly-bean machine in her stocking. The brightly-coloured beans were all different flavours: sweet, sour, super-fizzy. That's what the glow-stars smelled like: a super-fizzy, sour-sweet jelly bean that hadn't been invented yet.

The jelly-bean perfume and the rosy light made the attic feel more friendly; more like hers.

Jax was still drowsily gazing up at her glow-stars when the truth dawned. *They weren't pink.*

She sat up in a hurry. The flickering wasn't coming from her ceiling. She'd just assumed it was, like she'd just assumed her room was empty. She hadn't been thinking like a scientist. She wasn't thinking how a frightened alien would think.

Jax couldn't hear the radio station now, just her own excited breathing. She quickly slipped out of bed. Now she'd got her scientist's head on, she was able to make out shimmery marks on her carpet, like the ones she'd spotted on the stairs. She studied the little marks more closely. The harder she looked, the less they looked like footprints. Jax thought they looked more like paw prints.

They stopped abruptly beside her bed. It was obvious now where the pink flickering was coming from.

It was coming from under her bed.

Jax was so excited she was shaking. She took a deep breath to calm herself, and got ready to meet her first alien.

She inched forward, peering cautiously under her bed, and immediately had to shield her eyes. It was like looking into the heart of a dazzling star, a star that fizzed and flickered with a rosy light.

The fizzy light must be coming from the alien, she thought.

But though her eyes gradually adjusted, she could only see the light; she still couldn't see the alien. *Maybe it doesn't want to be seen*, she thought. "Oh, *I* get it!" she breathed. "You weren't sure it was safe, so you made yourself invisible."

Jax saw a tiny movement where the light

was brightest. A second ago there was nothing there. Now, a small huddled *something* shyly uncurled and stretched.

Can you see me now?

Jax blinked and gasped. She was looking into a pair of amber-gold eyes. At the same moment, she heard a loud sneeze from the landing.

Jax only had one thought in her head: *Mum mustn't see the alien.* Before she had time to think, she yanked it out from under the bed, stuffing it inside her cardigan. There was no scientific reason for an alien to resemble a human, Dad had told her, so Jax was prepared for just about anything; something cold, slippery, maybe even scaly? (She *really* hoped it didn't have long waving tentacles.) But this alien was warm and soft to touch, and much smaller than she'd imagined.

When her mum walked in, Jax was doing her best to look normal.

"Hi, Mum," she said cheerfully.

Her mum stared down at her in surprise. "What are you doing crawling around on the floor? You said you were going to bed!"

Jax was alarmed to notice a telltale pink flicker coming from inside her cardigan. "I lost my torch," she invented frantically. "I just found it, look!" She waved it wildly, so Mum would think all the pink fizzing and flickering was coming from her torch.

"Why do you need your torch if you're going to sleep?" Mum asked suspiciously.

"I don't *need* it. I like to keep it by my bed for emergencies." Jax could feel the alien's tiny heart beating quickly against hers. It was such a strange feeling that she almost laughed out loud.

To Jax's relief, her mum was overtaken by another sneeze and had to dash off to find her inhaler. "And switch that – *ASHOO!* – light off!" she called irritably.

The light wasn't on. It was the alien's pink lightning that Mum could see. But Jax just said meekly, "Okay, Mum, night!" and dived beneath her covers with the alien. It seemed to know it had to stay quiet, because it didn't make even a tiny squeak.

At last Mum went hurrying downstairs, still sneezing. Carefully keeping under the covers, Jax unbuttoned her cardigan, and set the little creature free. Under the pinkly glowing tent of her duvet, Jax and the alien came face-to-face at last.

"No way," she breathed. "You're a *kitten!*"

There's a comical in-between stage that kittens go through, where they all look like space aliens even when they're not. The alien kitten was going through that stage. Its lanky legs seemed to belong to a different, taller cat, and its golden eyes were ridiculously huge for its tiny pointed face. It looked almost like a normal marmalade kitten, Jax thought, except for the starry glints and sparkles in its fur.

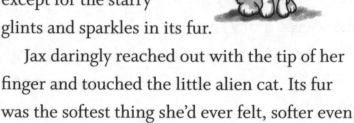

Jax daringly reached out with the tip of her finger and touched the little alien cat. Its fur was the softest thing she'd ever felt, softer even than Mum's precious cashmere sweater.

It seemed to Jax that she had waited for this moment her whole life. "I *knew* I'd find you one day!" she whispered. "Did you know you'd find me?"

The kitten blinked its intelligent golden

eyes. *At first I knew, but after I landed I got mixed up. Your planet is a very mixing-up kind of planet.*

"I can hear your thoughts!" Jax breathed. She had heard the kitten's words inside her mind as clear as day. *Wow,* she thought. The kids at school would see her talking to birds on telephone wires and be amazed!

You can't talk to all animals, just me, the kitten explained.

Jax gasped. "You can hear *my* thoughts too!"

I can hear them because you're my human.

Jax thought she'd test this out. *Are you a boy cat or a girl cat?* she wondered silently.

The kitten seemed surprised. *I'm a boy of course!*

They were actually mind-talking! Jax hugged herself with delight. Then she had a new and thrilling thought. "Did you...erm...I suppose you didn't just come to our planet to meet me?"

Jax felt herself turning red. Now the kitten would think she was really big-headed.

But he seemed to think this was a perfectly sensible question. *The Aunts said you had to help me with my mission.*

Jax felt as if she must be dreaming, yet she knew this was really happening. "Did the Aunts tell you my name?" she asked shyly. "I'm called Ellie Mae Jackson, but everyone calls me Jax."

The kitten's tail gave a satisfied swish, as if this was the exact name he'd expected to hear. Jax waited for him to tell her his name in return. *We don't use names on our planet*, he told her.

A world with no names sounded confusing to Jax. "Would it be okay if I make up a name for you?" she asked.

He thought for a moment. *I'd have to ask the Aunts.*

It was the second time he'd mentioned his mysterious aunts. *They can't be actual aunt-type aunts,* Jax thought. *They must be like some alien organization.*

The kitten was gradually creeping closer. Fitting himself carefully into the exact crook of her arm, he started to purr. Jax decided alien cats had a more complicated purr than Earth cats. The lower notes reminded her of a tea kettle slowly coming to a bubbling boil. The top notes sounded like crowds of tiny songbirds, all singing different tunes. It was the happiest, most soothing sound she had ever heard.

Jax heard a sudden *"ASHOO!"* Mum was coming back upstairs.

The kitten stopped purring, looking wild-eyed. *What will she do to me if she finds me?*

"She wouldn't do anything!" Jax whispered, horrified. "My mum would never hurt you. It's just that I'm not supposed to have a kitten for a pet."

The kitten's eyes instantly narrowed.

Jax felt herself turning red. "That was the wrong word," she said apologetically. "You're not a pet. I know that. You're, like, my guest. You're just staying with me until you've completed your mission. But my mum totally mustn't know you're here, okay?"

A new worry crossed her mind; even Brad the goldfish had to poo. "Will you need, um, a litter tray?" she asked anxiously.

The kitten's eyes blazed up like amber flames before she had finished her sentence. She hadn't wanted him to be embarrassed, that's all, but now it was Jax who was embarrassed. She was just wishing that the floor would open up and swallow her for ever, when the kitten gave her wrist a quick lick with his rough little tongue. Jax knew she was forgiven, because he was purring his tea-kettle purr again.

The fizzy pink flickering was hardly noticeable now. *He's adjusting*, she thought. *He's adjusting to being on our planet.*

Jax stroked the kitten's silky-soft fur and made a surprise discovery. When she brushed it the wrong way, she could see moonlight-coloured tiger stripes underneath.

I'm a moon cat, the kitten explained. *All moon cats have them.*

Jax was amazed. "Are there seriously cats living on the moon?" She pictured them prowling through a lunar underground city, hidden from the prying eyes of spy satellites.

Not your moon, the kitten corrected, *a moon in a far away galaxy. Moon cats have been taking an interest in your planet for thousands of*  years. *In olden times, we were worshipped as gods.*

"Like in ancient Egypt," Jax breathed. She had learned about ancient Egyptians at her old school.

The kitten yawned, showing his pink tongue. Jax yawned in sympathy. She hadn't had a proper night's sleep since they moved.

She snuggled drowsily under her covers. She hoped the kitten would curl up beside her, but he went plodding up and down her quilt for ages, looking for a comfortable position. At last he settled for wrapping himself very carefully around her head, like a small furry hat.

Having a purring kitten on your head was

44

surprisingly comforting. Jax felt her eyelids growing heavy. She was drifting off to sleep when she suddenly snapped wide awake again. She had thought of the perfect name for her moon kitten.

"Can I call you Moonbeans?" she whispered.

What are "moonbeans"? The kitten seemed puzzled.

"It's like a joke," she explained. "You're a moon cat, and it sounds almost like moon*beams*! Plus you smell like the loveliest jelly beans ever."

Describe "jelly beans", said the kitten.

"They're a kind of sweet. They're delicious," Jax explained.

Humans like them?

"Human kids love them."

I will ask the Aunts. Without warning, the kitten launched himself off her head. In a single bound, he had reached her window sill.

Jax clutched at her scalp. "Ow! Mind your claws!"

Through her bare window, she could see a tiny pale star winking above the rooftops. Gazing intensely at the star, the kitten began to purr. This wasn't the tea-kettle purr or the choir of little birds, but a new, strangely urgent sound that made the whole room vibrate. Jax felt herself starting to tingle all over.

Brad swam up to the surface of his tank, shivering his tiny fins, as if he wondered what was going on. The room began to shimmer with a now-familiar fiery pink light. Jax held her breath. Was the kitten actually *purring* a message to a distant planet?

Jax couldn't tell how long the purred transmission went on. At last it finished, and the kitten hopped back onto her pillow. He started washing, as if nothing unusual had happened.

"Did the Aunts get your message?" Jax still didn't totally believe he had spoken to them.

The kitten seemed surprised that she should even ask. *Of course! They say Moonbeans is a very good name.*

"That's really all you did?" Jax breathed. "You just purred and they could hear you – thousands of light years away?"

Millions, the kitten corrected, *millions of light years.*

"That can't be science," Jax said doubtfully. "It's got to be magic."

The kitten stopped in mid-wash. *On my planet, science and magic are the same thing.*

Jax thought this was the most thrilling idea she'd ever heard. Her dad would have loved it!

She was never going to get to
sleep now, what with her
room full of zingy pink
lightning and all these
exciting new thoughts buzzing
round her head. Not to mention the fact that
she had no idea what she was going to do with
Moonbeans when she started back at school.

School doesn't start till Monday, she
remembered with relief. She still had Sunday
to figure everything out. She'd have a whole
day with Moonbeans. Lulled by the soothing
music of a moon cat's purr, Jax drifted off to
sleep in a room that was still quietly fizzing
with magic.

Sunrise with Moonbeans

4

Jax was being pulled up through fuzzy layers of sleep. She let out a whimper, burrowing back under her covers, desperate to stay inside her dream. It was the loveliest dream she had ever had in her life and she couldn't bear for it to stop. Towards the end, a golden-eyed kitten had been gently patting her face. To her surprise, Jax could still feel her cheek being patted, only now there was the tiniest hint of claw.

She sat up in a hurry and found herself staring into a pair of amber-gold eyes.

Everything suddenly flooded back: glow-stars that smelled of jelly beans, pink lightning under her bed… "Oh, Moonbeans, you're real," she breathed. "I thought you were a dream!"

Jax suddenly caught sight of her clock radio. "You didn't have to wake me so early," she complained. "It isn't morning for ages."

I want to see the sun rise. Don't you want to watch it with me? The kitten seemed disappointed.

Jax didn't, not on a Sunday – not at all in fact. Then she remembered. Moonbeans was her guest from a far-off star system. This was his first day on a strange planet. Dad would want her to be hospitable. Still yawning, she put on her dressing gown. She would watch the sun come up, to please Moonbeans, then go back to bed for a little snooze.

Moonbeans was already in position on her window sill. He fixed his eyes expectantly on a point above the rooftops, just as the first birds began to twitter. Jax dutifully went to join him.

As the pale light of a new day stole across the rooftops, something unexpected happened. Jax started to feel oddly excited. She felt as if she was seeing Earth's dawn for the first time too, like Moonbeans.

I'm probably the only child in Goose Green who's watching this, she realized. She wanted to say this to Moonbeans, but he was sitting so still he seemed to be in a trance. The only part of him that moved was the very slightly twitching tip of his tail.

When he finally turned to her, the little moon cat's eyes seemed bigger and more golden than ever. *Now you may talk.*

"Is our dawn different to dawn on your planet?" she asked.

He blinked at her. *Yes, because it has singing.*

"Singing? Oh, you mean the *birds*! Don't you have birds then?"

We have them, but moon birds don't sing.

"Moon birds? Honestly?" Jax hugged herself at the very idea. *Wow, I wonder what moon birds look like*, she thought.

She didn't feel the least bit sleepy now. She felt super-wide awake. "Don't know about you, Beans, but I'm starving!"

He delicately washed a paw. *You called me Beans, not Moonbeans.*

"'Beans is like your nickname," Jax explained. "Like, my full name is a real mouthful, so people call me Jax for short."

Jax and Beans. It sounds funny.

Jax wasn't sure but she thought the moon kitten was smiling. She laughed. "We'll be like the amazing duo: Jax and Beans! So what would you like for breakfast, Beans?"

I would like some jelly beans.

Just in time, she saw the glint in his eye. Beans was joking.

"I'll be right back," she told him.

A few minutes later, Jax returned with a tray. "It's not jelly beans, but crunchy cereal is almost as good!" She set everything out carefully on her rug.

Beans seemed to enjoy their dawn picnic, munching cereal, and carefully lapping water from a saucer. He must have liked it, because he washed his whiskers for ages afterwards.

When he'd finished washing, Beans set off to explore her room.

He peered closely at the framed photos beside her bed.

Jax got ready to say, *Oh, that's my dad, he's dead*, but to her relief the kitten had already moved on to the next photo. "That's me doing karate at my old school," she explained.

You look scary, as if you're going to fight somebody!

She laughed. "I'm supposed to look like that."

Moonbeans was studying the last photograph. *That's the human who sneezes. Why does she sneeze all the time?*

Jax could have told the truth: *Because she's allergic to cats.* Instead, she said airily, "Who knows? My mum's allergic to, like, the *entire* universe." She was slightly shocked at herself for being so mean.

I don't care, Jax thought stubbornly. Mum had made her give up everything: her home, her friends, even her grandpa. Well, she wasn't giving up Moonbeans.

The moon kitten was investigating her old rainbow-coloured slinky. Without warning, he tossed it into the air, the way Jax had seen cats play with a mouse. The slinky landed on its coiled base, then took off like a wild springy caterpillar, somersaulting across the room, with Beans madly chasing it all around, until kitten and slinky both came to rest in a breathless tangle. Jax had to stuff her pillow over her face, she was laughing so hard. It was the first time she'd seen Moonbeans play like a normal kitten.

He had a quick wash to recover his dignity, then, to her alarm, he jumped onto her desk, heading straight for Brad's tank.

"Oh, don't—" Jax started – then stopped, amazed, as her fish swam up to the surface of his tank, letting out a stream of silvery bubbles.

Beans turned to Jax. *He says he is honoured to share his human with me.*

Jax shot a doubtful glance at Brad. "He seriously said all that?"

She heard a distant sneeze. Mum was finally getting up.

"Can you make yourself invisible again?" she begged Beans.

For some reason he was suddenly avoiding her eyes. *I'd rather not. Open the window and I'll go for a walk.*

Jax managed to push up the old-fashioned sash window and Beans slipped out. She felt a sudden rush of panic. "Do be careful," she called after him in a hoarse whisper. "Some humans aren't actually that nice."

She was too late. The moon kitten was already picking his way along the fire escapes at the backs of the houses. Jax held her breath until she saw him land safely in a neighbour's garden.

She found her mum in the kitchen, whipping up pancake batter.

"I'm making us a proper breakfast for a change." Mum's voice was painfully croaky. *She looks really poorly*, Jax thought with a pang.

"Maybe you're allergic to mice?" she suggested guiltily. "You're allergic to fur, and mice are *kind* of furry."

Mum shuddered. "Don't even talk about them," she croaked. "Thank goodness the mouse man is coming tomorrow."

Jax had discovered that getting up at dawn makes you starving hungry. She demolished her second breakfast in no time, even helping her mum to finish hers.

"Better get back to cleaning," Mum said huskily. "You've got to organize your things for tomorrow, don't forget."

"You don't have to nag!" Jax snapped. She was being grumpy because she knew she was being selfish. She should help Mum with the cleaning, but then she'd miss out on her special day with Moonbeans.

 Jax watched her mum trudge downstairs, clutching a fresh bottle of the extra-strong cleaning liquid they'd found on special offer. The liquid was a dangerous shade of green, like a wizard's evil potion, and smelled like something you'd use to clear drains.

The minute she heard scrubbing sounds starting up, Jax hurried back to her room.

Beans had returned from his walk, looking pleased with himself.

I made friends with an Earth cat, he told her, *an old warrior cat. His ears are tattered and torn. His name is Rumble.*

Jax wrinkled her nose. "Is *that* what he's called?" She had seen the battered old tomcat sleeping on their shed roof. "He smells like old fish," she complained.

He says he told the other cats about me. He knew I would come.

She laughed. "He's having you on! No way could that stinky old cat know about cats from other galaxies!"

He is stinky, but wise and kind. He says he will help me.

Jax was hurt. "I thought you said you needed my help?"

I do need your help, with my mission, Beans explained calmly.

"Oh, I see," said Jax, who didn't see at all. She waited for Beans to explain what he needed Rumble's help for.

But he simply changed the subject. *Tell me about the man in the photo.*

Taken by surprise, Jax felt her eyes sting with tears. She tried to make her voice ordinary. "Oh, that's my dad."

He's the man who loved the stars?

Jax gasped. "How did you know?"

I think maybe because you're my human.

Jax could have cried with relief. Beans understood.

60

She took a shaky breath. "My dad was a scientist. He totally believed there were intelligent beings on other planets. I think that's why I've always dreamed of meeting one."

Beans didn't answer straight away. *Now I know why the Aunts sent me to you,* he said at last. *I always had that dream too.*

"That is *so* spooky," Jax breathed. "Two of us living in different galaxies and having the exact same dream. Were you lonely too? I was *really* lonely before you came."

Is lonely like unhappy?

"It's worse. It feels like you're trapped inside a little bubble all by yourself, and nobody would notice if you weren't even there."

Your mum would notice.

Jax gave an angry laugh. "All she cares about is this dirty old café. I mean, it's got mice, can you believe that? Mum's got to get a man in from the council."

What will he do? Beans asked.

"Kill them, of course. You can't have mice where people are eating."

Beans looked appalled. *Why doesn't she just ask the mice to go away?*

Jax laughed, then realized he was serious. "Humans often talk to cats and dogs," she admitted. "But I never heard of anyone talking to a mouse!"

I will talk to them, said Beans. *I'll explain that they must find a new home.*

"That would be great," Jax said politely, not really believing him.

One of Beans's feathery ears gave an anxious twitch. *Your mum is coming.*

For the first time ever, Jax was grateful for Mum's allergies. Her sneezes acted like an early-warning system, giving Beans plenty of time to dive out of sight.

Beans had to do a lot of hiding as the day went on.

"It would be easier if you turned invisible," Jax suggested several times. But each time the kitten avoided her eyes and said firmly that he'd rather not.

The minute her mum disappeared back downstairs, Jax and Moonbeans would carry on chatting. Jax didn't think she'd ever talked to anyone the way she talked to Beans. The day just whizzed by. In no time, it seemed to her, lights were coming on in the backs of the neighbours' houses. Jax reluctantly started to get her school things ready. Tomorrow she was going to have to put on this ugly bottle-green uniform and walk into a playground full of strangers. The thought made her want to run and hide. Then she thought, *Beans must have been super-scared before he blasted off to Earth, and he's just a little moon kitten.* If Beans could be brave, so could she.

She could feel Moonbeans watching her with interest as she hung her school clothes carefully on her chair and put her brand-new pencils, rubber and ruler in her school bag.

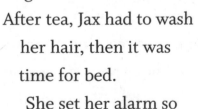

After tea, Jax had to wash her hair, then it was time for bed.

She set her alarm so she could get up to catch the dawn with Beans. Mum came in to kiss her goodnight. Jax secretly pulled a face. Her mum was starting to *smell* like cut-price cleaning fluid.

"Don't worry about tomorrow, sweetie, you'll soon make new friends," Mum croaked, switching off Jax's lamp.

Jax smiled to herself in the dark. She had a mind-reading moon cat. Why would she need friends?

"You can come out now, Beans," she whispered.

At 5.30 a.m. on the dot, Jax's alarm went off with a loud jangle.

She sat up, excited and wide awake, ready to repeat yesterday's dawn magic. "Beans?"

He wasn't there.

Her window was closed. Jax had left it open to let Beans come and go. Mum must have shut it in the night, trapping the moon kitten outside.

She padded to her window and peered out. It was raining heavily. He'd get soaked. She wasn't sure if they even had rain on his planet.

At last she spotted him in a nearby garden, and was surprised to see that Beans had a companion: a fire-red, long-nosed animal, with a tail like a brush. Mum said urban  foxes were a menace. They raided rubbish bins and caused havoc in people's gardens. Beans didn't seem to feel the same way. He and the fox were acting like old friends. She pushed up the window. "Beans!" she called softly. "I'm awake! You can come back now!" But he didn't look up.

Jax decided she wasn't that bothered about watching the sun rise, not if Beans couldn't be bothered to come back. Feeling sorry for herself, she crawled under her covers and accidentally went back to sleep.

When Mum woke her, two hours later, Jax was confused. Had the rainy garden and the fire-red fox just been a dream? And where was Moonbeans?

He still hadn't returned by the time she had to leave for school.

Jax looked out for him anxiously as she and Mum splashed through the rain puddles. The gloomy weather made the day so dark that the cars all had their lights on. She should have warned Moonbeans to be careful on the roads. *He'll be okay,* she told herself bravely. *I expect he's on his way home right this minute.* Moonbeans wasn't one of those fluffy pyjama-case cats who snooze the day away. He'd probably been out gathering info for his mission.

Goose Green Primary School was airy and modern. Jax's new class teacher, Mrs. Chaudhary, had jet-black hair with dramatic streaks of white.

"You can sit with Lilia," Mrs. Chaudhary told her, smiling. "Lilia only moved to Goose Green a few months ago and she's settling in really well."

A boy at the next table said something rude under his breath.

"That's enough, Conrad." From her tired expression, Jax could tell that Mrs. Chaudhary had to say this to Conrad a lot.

Jax glanced at the window, feeling trapped, picturing herself jumping out and running back to Moonbeans. First she'd have to fight her way through a display of home-made mobiles made from recycled materials. *I shan't see Beans for*

hours and hours, she thought miserably. If she could have just seen him before she left, she wouldn't feel so bad.

Jax felt Lilia nudging her with her elbow. "Is it your mum who's doing up Dolly's Diner?" Lilia asked her shyly.

"She's wasting her time," Conrad jeered. "No one wants your mum's fancy-pants café. We all liked Dolly's how it was before."

"If you can't behave, you will have to come and sit with me," Mrs. Chaudhary told him. Conrad shut his mouth and immediately started jiggling his foot. Jax had been in his class for five minutes and she was tired of Conrad already. His red hair stood up in spikes, and he had the most freckles she had ever seen on one person.

Jax cautiously looked around the room and was embarrassed to see the two children she had spied on through Dad's telescope. *I was a different person then*, she told herself. *That was before Moonbeans.*

Mrs. Chaudhary had started taking the register. The floppy-haired boy's name was Howard. The tap-dancing girl was called Ruby-Rose. Jax might have guessed she'd be called something sparkly.

She wished she could fast-forward to home time. Moonbeans should be back by then. *It's only natural that he wants to explore*, she thought. To Beans, our planet probably seemed super-new and exciting.

Jax felt herself flush with shame as she realized that she had spent all day with Moonbeans without ever once asking him about his mission. *I bet my dad would have asked right away*, she thought guiltily. *I just wanted me and Beans to hide away together in our own private little world.*

She felt a flicker of worry. What if she'd upset Moonbeans? What if he'd gone off to find a nicer, more thoughtful human child to help him with his mission?

She had started doodling pictures of cats and kittens in her workbook without noticing. Lilia leaned over to look. "We've got two kittens," she whispered. "They're magic."

Not as magic as mine, thought Jax and she almost burst into tears. *I'll do anything*, she prayed desperately. *Just please let Moonbeans be there when I get home.*

At break, Jax stood by herself in the playground.

Ruby-Rose and Lilia were playing a skipping game with a gang of other girls. Jax could hear

Ruby-Rose chanting,
"*In* comes the doctor,
in comes the nurse,"
as she turned the rope.

Lilia shyly came over. "Want to play?"

Jax shook her head. She wasn't interested in making new friends. She just wanted to go home to Moonbeans.

Conrad was watching them with a funny little smirk on his face.

"Keep away from that boy," Lilia whispered. "He does karate."

"I do karate too, so he should keep away from me," said Jax in a cross voice. Lilia gave a nervous giggle. She thought Jax was joking.

At lunchtime, Jax finally got to see Conrad doing his "karate". He danced around the playground, aiming wild kicks at Lilia, shouting

"Ha!" like a ninja. "Don't look so scared!" he taunted. "I'll stop as soon as you say 'please'. Say, 'Please, *pleeeease*, Conrad, don't hurt me.'"

Jax did some quick thinking. She had told Lilia the truth. She really had studied karate at her old school. But her teacher always insisted that they must never ever use it to hurt anyone. (Plus Mum would go nuts if Jax got into a playground fight on her very first day!)

No one likes a snitch, but nobody else was doing anything to help Lilia, so Jax ran to get a teacher. Conrad was marched off to Mr. Tattersall's office. When he came back to their class, he was still smirking.

He thinks he's so clever, Jax thought.

She stole a look at Lilia, who had salty tear tracks on her cheeks. Lilia was pale to begin with, but now she was upset she was extra-specially pale. Before she had time to think, Jax gave her a nudge. "Conrad's just a big show-off," she whispered. "That wasn't even proper karate. It's just something he's made up."

Lilia's eyes went wide. "Can you do real karate?"

"Loads of girls did it at my old school," Jax told her airily.

For the rest of the afternoon, Lilia kept staring at Jax as if she had just crashed to Earth from another planet, like Moonbeans.

Conrad was staring at Jax too, but with a totally different expression. Jax thought he was imagining himself aiming wild karate kicks at her, shouting, "Say *pleeeease*, Ellie Mae!" She silently carried on with her long divisions, ignoring them both.

At last it was home time. Jax tried to hurry

her mum along, but she kept stopping to sneeze or blow her nose. Jax noticed people giving them unfriendly looks. She remembered Conrad's sneers about no one wanting Mum's café and hunched her shoulders, wishing she could turn invisible like Moonbeans. *Does she have to sneeze so loudly?* Jax thought, embarrassed.

Her mum didn't seem to notice the stares. She was so carried away with her plans for renovating Dolly's Diner, it didn't occur to her that some local people liked it the way it was.

"How did your day go?" Mum asked.

Jax shrugged. "Okay."

So Mum started telling Jax about her day, which had left her totally puzzled. The mouse man had turned up with his bag of poisoned crumbs, but when he went into the storeroom, there was no sign the mice had ever been there!

Jax managed to hide her little gasp of surprise. Beans had promised he'd talk to the mice, but she hadn't believed him! And that meant he must have come home.

As they hurried over the pedestrian crossing with a crowd of parents and kids, Jax had such an overwhelming need to see her moon kitten that she couldn't wait even one more minute.

"I could see the man thought I was completely – *ASHOO!* – barking mad! Jax, are you even listening?" her mum complained.

Jax started to run.

"Where's the fire!" joked one of the dads.

She ignored him, putting on an extra spurt, dodging around baby buggies and toddlers, jumping over puddles, speeding past the launderette with its strong smell of hot soap, hurrying home to Moonbeans.

Jax found the little moon cat curled up on her bed, fast asleep in a patch of sunlight. She buried her face in his fur. He smelled of sunshine and very faintly of jelly beans. She gave a little sob of relief.

Beans stretched sleepily. *What's wrong?*

"I was so scared you wouldn't come back! I thought you'd gone to find some other human to live with."

Beans seemed puzzled. *But you're my human! The Aunts sent me to you.*

"But I don't deserve you," Jax wailed. "I keep

making you hide from Mum and I never even asked about your mission. I'm a horrible, selfish girl."

I've got a confession too, Moonbeans said unexpectedly. *I didn't tell you the whole truth about why I came to Earth.*

Jax blinked away her tears. She wasn't sure what Beans was trying to tell her. "Was the mission part not true then?"

The mission part was true.

Jax was just getting ready to ask Moonbeans what his mission was, when he said shyly, *But I've got another reason for wanting to visit your planet – a secret reason that even the Aunts don't know about.*

Jax had to hide a smile. She didn't want to hurt his feelings, but she couldn't imagine what kind of secret such a little kitten could possibly have.

I want to find my dad, Beans told her.

Jax was astonished. "Isn't your dad a moon cat?"

No, said Beans. *He's from your world.*

She pulled a face. "Don't tell me Rumble is your dad?"

It isn't Rumble, Beans said with dignity. *Stop talking for a minute and I'll tell you what happened.*

Jax solemnly zipped her lips and settled down to listen.

A few years ago, a delegation of moon cats travelled to Earth on a fact-finding expedition. They wanted to see if there was any way they could help the life forms on your planet to live happier lives. Beans gave her an apologetic lick. *Moon cats think of your world as being slightly backward,* he explained. Then he quickly went on with his story.

During their trip, the moon cats spent several days in Goose Green. One balmy midsummer's night, one of the female cats met an extremely *handsome local cat. They were two cats from different galaxies, yet they fell head over heels in love.*

"Oh, Beans that is so romantic," Jax breathed.

My mum knew it could never last, Beans said wistfully, *but after she returned home she had five beautiful kittens.*

Jax quickly counted on her fingers. "Sorry, Beans, but that doesn't add up. You said it happened years ago, but you're still just a kitten."

On my world, kittens stay kittens for much longer.

"But can cats from two different worlds really have kittens?"

The Aunts believe such kittens have special magic gifts. My four sisters are all very talented. Beans suddenly got busy washing his tail.

"What about your magic gifts?" she asked at once.

Beans seemed to be concentrating extra hard on his tail.

"Beans?"

The Aunts say I'm a late bloomer, he confessed. *In our invisibility test, I got stuck being invisible. The Aunts had to turn me back.*

Jax remembered how she couldn't see the moon kitten when he first arrived. "Were you stuck being invisible when you were hiding under my bed?"

Yes. Then you talked to me and unstuck me.

"Did I?" Jax said amazed. "How did I do that?"

It was your voice, Beans explained. *It made me feel safe so I could turn myself visible again.*

"That's why you had to hide every time Mum came upstairs! Oh, poor little Beans." Jax tenderly stroked his head. She could tell he felt totally humiliated.

The Aunts met together to discuss what to do about me. They think that because I'm half Earth cat, I needed to come to Earth before my magic would start working properly, and then I can carry out their mission.

This time Jax jumped right in with her question. "What *is* the Aunts' mission, Beans?" she asked politely.

He blinked in surprise. *To help the life forms of Goose Green, of course.*

"Help life forms how?" she asked.

Help them to be happy, I already told you that. Beans rubbed up against her shoulder. *I'm*

proud the Aunts have given me such an important mission, he confided, *but while I'm here I really hope I can find my dad.*

Jax totally understood. If her dad was alive and living on a strange planet, she would want to find him too. She had a sudden thought. "Have you done any magic today?"

Not today, no, Beans said after a pause.

"Why not?" Jax demanded. "Don't you want to know if coming to Earth has improved your magic powers, like the Aunts said?"

What if it hasn't, though? Beans's eyes were huge with worry.

"Turn yourself invisible," she ordered. "Don't think. Just do it!"

Beans obediently sat down and closed his eyes.

Jax shut her eyes in sympathy, willing the magic to work. Then she cautiously opened half an eye.

No Beans.

In just two tiny heartbeats, he'd turned himself invisible.

Jax clapped and cheered. "Yay, Beans! Now quickly come back on a count of three. One, two—"

Before she got to "three", Beans reappeared. His fur was fluffed out as if he'd been blow-dried. He frantically tried to lick it back to normal. *Urgh*, he shuddered.

Poor Beans, Jax thought. He'd obviously been dreading getting stuck again. "I *know* you hated it," Jax said sympathetically. "But you DID it! Now you've got to practise like crazy until you can turn invisible without thinking."

I've got an idea, said Beans, when his fur had finally subsided.

When Jax heard Beans's idea, she hugged him until he squeaked.

Next morning, as she walked to school with an invisible moon kitten peeping out of her bag, Jax learned an interesting new fact. Birds and animals aren't taken in by invisibility; nor are very young children.

After a few minutes, wondering what all the commotion was about, her mum glanced behind them and saw a dream-like procession; dogs dragging their owners along on their leads, toddlers pointing from their buggies, cats peering down, fascinated, from the tops of walls. Birds zipped to and fro across the street,

shouting out the news.
One blackbird
zoomed around Jax's
head in a circle, then
flew off into the children's
playground, chattering excitedly.

Mum was bewildered. "What *is* going on?"

A Border collie ran up and rapturously
sniffed at Jax's bag. "I don't know what's got
into him!" his owner said apologetically. He
dragged his dog away, the collie still wildly
wagging its tail.

It was a relief to run into school, away from
all the attention.

"I don't think this is such a good idea. Some
of those little kids could see you!" she hissed
into her bag.

Only the very little ones, Beans said calmly.
Something happens to humans after they start

school, the Aunts said. They start only seeing with their eyes.

Jax was confused. "Most people see with their eyes, don't they?"

Moon cats see with their whole hearts, said Beans.

Feeling more confused than ever, Jax set her bag down on the floor. "All right, you can go exploring, but don't draw attention to yourself, okay," she whispered.

But she quickly saw that Beans was right. No one in her class had the slightest suspicion that an invisible moon kitten was prowling around their classroom.

Beans was so well behaved during their first lesson that Jax almost forgot he was there. Halfway through the next lesson, which was English, she heard silvery tinkling sounds. Her teacher gave a puzzled glance towards the

display of mobiles in the
window. The window
was closed and there
was no breeze, but all
the mobiles were
suddenly spinning wildly.

"Beans, cut that out!" Jax hissed.

Beans obediently stopped batting at
the mobiles and went back to exploring.
Occasionally he came to sit by her feet, curling
his tail around her ankles as he reported back
about the kids in her class.

*Lilia's mum just got divorced, that's why they
moved to Goose Green. Conrad's dad is away on
the oil rigs. Conrad has two older brothers and
three little brothers, so his mum is usually too busy
to give him much attention.*

Jax didn't care about Conrad or his mum
and dad. Conrad was a show-off and a bully. I'm

Beans's special human, not Lilia or Conrad, she thought jealously. How come he could read these other kids' thoughts?

I don't know how I can read their thoughts. Beans seemed apologetic. *Being on Earth must be strengthening my magic powers, like the Aunts said.*

The last lesson of the morning was silent reading. They just had ten minutes left when Jax heard shrill squeals from the back of the class. She slid down in her seat, wishing she could disappear. Beans must be introducing himself to the class guinea pigs.

Mrs. Chaudhary marched over to the cage, pretending to be cross. "Shush! This is supposed to be SILENT reading!"

The squealing stopped as if by magic.

The children stared at their teacher with open mouths.

"I never knew you spoke guinea pig, miss," Conrad said cheekily and everyone howled with laughter.

Sorry, Beans said humbly when he and Jax were alone in the playground. *I didn't know the guinea pigs would be so happy to meet me.*

Jax was getting the impression that every cat, dog, bird, creepy-crawly (and probably *germ*) in Goose Green was delighted to meet Moonbeans; and big-hearted Moonbeans loved them all right back! This was not how she'd pictured life with a magical moon cat. She'd imagined it being her and Beans against the world. She never dreamed the world would expect her to *share* him!

Beans had been trying to attract her attention. "Hmm?" she said.

I think Lilia is in trouble.

Conrad was loping towards Lilia, with his lopsided little smirk. Lilia stood rooted to the spot, looking terrified, not knowing what to do.

Someone should teach that boy a lesson, Jax thought fiercely. Then she gasped. She'd had a brilliant idea. "Beans! You could use your moon magic on Conrad! You know you need the practice," she added cunningly.

Beans thought for a minute. *I'll try, but you have to help.*

Jax laughed. "I can't do magic!"

No, but you can do karate. Show Conrad your scariest karate move and I'll try to give him a surprise he won't forget.

Conrad was jeering at Lilia again. "All you've got to do is say '*Pleeeease*'."

93

Beans had only said he'd try, Jax realized. That meant he still wasn't a hundred per cent confident of his magic powers. If this didn't work, she was going to embarrass herself big-time.

Just go for it, Jax, she told herself, swallowing.

The next minute, she was running straight at Conrad, yelling at the top of her voice, "You think you can do karate, do you? Well, look and learn, little boy!" And she did her best flying karate kick.

To her and everyone's amazement, hot-pink lightning came flashing from her hands and feet, followed by tiny shooting stars of all colours. For a split second, Jax was a starry, flashing, kicking, punching human firework

– then she landed in front of Conrad with a grin of triumph, and she was a normal girl again.

She hadn't even touched Conrad, but he backed away from her, wide-eyed. "No WAY."

Jax quickly dusted off her hands. They felt uncomfortably tingly, but she wasn't going to let Conrad know that.

"How did you—?" he asked shakily. "It was just a trick, right? Yeah, it was just a trick," he repeated to himself. He shook his head, totally dazed. "No way was that for real," he whispered.

"You go on thinking that if it makes you feel better," Jax said airily. "Come on, Lilia, let's go." She hooked her arm through Lilia's and the two girls walked away.

To her surprise, Conrad ran after them. "Will you teach me to do that?" he begged.

Jax gave a scornful laugh. "What, so you can bully girls?"

"Not the kick, the little stars." Conrad's face was pleading. "Go on, Ellie," he wheedled. "Look, I'm sorry, all right! I wasn't ever going to hurt her. I go a bit bonkers sometimes that's all. Show me how you did it. Please?"

Jax noticed that Conrad had said "please" in a quieter, more normal voice, not how he'd said it when he was teasing and taunting Lilia.

Thanks, Beans, Jax thought. How was she going to talk her way out of this?

"Actually the stars were a one-off," she said, thinking fast. "I was mad with you for bullying Lilia, that's what did it."

Conrad's eyes went wide. "You mean you got, like, temporary super powers?"

She shrugged. "Something like that."

He gave a nervous laugh. "I'll try to remember not to make you mad, then!"

"All kinds of things make me mad," Jax said

coolly. "Being mean about my mum's café, for one. Have you got that, Conrad?"

"Got it." Conrad gulped, and slowly mooched away.

Jax puffed out her cheeks and decided to leave Beans at home in future. Mixing school and magic was just a bit *too* exciting.

For the rest of that afternoon, Jax could feel Lilia and Conrad staring at her. So were Howard, Ruby-Rose, and practically everyone else in her class.

As she walked home after school, some girls called, "Bye, Ellie!" as they ran by. Conrad ran past with two little freckle-faced boys that Jax guessed were his brothers. "Bye, Ellie," he mumbled.

"You're very popular today," Mum said, laughing.

Jax couldn't really explain that her classmates were just impressed by her temporary super powers. "How's the café going?" she asked, quickly changing the subject.

"The display cabinets arrived and I painted a small corner of the café yellow to see if I like the colour." She didn't sound too happy about it, Jax noticed.

"Are you okay, Mum?" she asked anxiously.

Mum pulled a face. "I've just had one of those days. I went into the post office and some pensioners in the queue were making remarks."

"Oh," said Jax.

"They used to be regulars at Dolly's." Her mum sighed. "They think my café is going to be too upscale for Goose Green. Then I rang your grandpa to tell him he'll be getting an invitation to our big launch, and he said not to count on him as he might be too busy." Mum tried to

98

smile. "I'm probably being silly. I suppose I thought he'd be proud of me for seeing something through for once."

For the first time, Jax felt a twinge of sympathy for her mum. All she wanted was to make a friendly café where people could come and enjoy themselves. But no one believed in her dream. Not even Grandpa!

Jax decided something had to be done.

"You know how you used your magic to help Lilia," she said to Beans that night before they settled down to sleep. "Could you use it to help my mum?"

What kind of help?

"You know, stop everyone being so mean."

Moon magic doesn't work like that, said Beans.

"Oh." Jax was disappointed.

I could do the Purr of Power, he suggested.

She spluttered with laughter. "The Purr of Power! What's *that*?"

Purring is extremely powerful if you do it right, Beans assured her.

Jax remembered the night Beans contacted the Aunts. Her room had been pink and fizzy for hours. If a moon cat's purr could travel millions of light years to a far distant galaxy, it should easily reach people in the same city.

I've never tried it with humans, Beans admitted. *You'd have to help.*

Jax giggled. "I don't know how to purr, silly!"

I'll do the purring part, he explained. *You just imagine that you're sending messages to everyone in Goose Green.*

"What kind of messages?"

That's up to you, Beans said.

He began to purr until the room was softly vibrating with the sound. The air gradually turned a deep fiery pink, then it began to flicker and flash.

Beans wasn't exaggerating, Jax thought. The Purr of Power was *REALLY* powerful. She could still see magical flashes even when she closed her eyes. Keeping her eyes tightly shut, Jax imagined tying neat handwritten messages onto balloons of all colours. All her messages said the same thing: *If you think Goose Green needs a good café, please help my mum to make it happen.*

When Jax had enough balloons, she let them float gracefully up into the sky over Goose Green, then pictured them dropping one by one through the rooftops into people's homes.

Towards the end, as she grew tired, it was harder to concentrate. For some reason her

thoughts kept going back to Grandpa. Jax quickly tied a new message to an imaginary lilac-coloured balloon.

Dear Grandpa,

Please come to Mum's launch. She needs you.

PS We love you and miss you loads.

She hadn't meant to add that last part, but as Jax pictured the balloon sailing away over the houses, carrying her message, her eyes prickled with tears because it was true.

The next day, Lilia was waiting for Jax in the school playground, holding an enormous box tied with shiny pink ribbon. "I told my mum that you stopped Conrad from bullying me and she made you these," she said. She held out the box.

Jax carefully untied the ribbon and peeped inside. Her eyes grew wide. Inside were the cutest cupcakes she had ever seen.

There were cupcakes like little nests, with blue birds perched on top; cakes like tiny flower gardens; cakes like little dollies'

hamburgers, down to the extra cheese and salad; there were woolly-looking baby lambs decorated with tiny marshmallows. Jax's favourite was a miniature tea-party cupcake. Somehow Lilia's mum had fitted in a teeny marzipan teapot, a cup, a saucer and a cherry-topped muffin on a teeny plate.

She peeked underneath the top layer and was amazed to see yet more cupcakes! "Your mum made all these?" Jax breathed.

"She used to work in a super-posh bakery," Lilia said. "She wants to run her own cupcake business, one day. That's, like, her big dream."

Like Mum and her café, thought Jax.

Before everyone went out at break, Jax offered the giant box of cupcakes around her class. Even Mrs. Chaudhary took one. Only Conrad stayed in his seat, jiggling his foot, looking everywhere except at the cupcakes.

He thinks he can't have one because he bullied Lilia, Jax thought. She pushed the box of cakes under his nose. "Take one," she said in a threatening voice, "or I'll get mad again."

Conrad gave her a surprised little grin. "Thanks," he said shyly.

Jax thought he'd go for the miniature hamburger, but he carefully picked out the last woolly lamb. Jax still had four cupcakes left over.

"I'll take them back for Mum," she told

Lilia. "She's stressing about getting the café painted in time for the launch."

She suddenly noticed Conrad listening. "What?" she snapped.

"Nothing," he mumbled. "I might know someone who can help, that's all."

At home time, Jax's mum was late coming to meet her. Lilia's mum offered to wait with Jax, but she shook her head. "Thanks, but she'll be here soon."

Jax waited until the playground was totally empty, then she started walking home, carrying the box with the leftover cupcakes. She had just reached the children's playground when she saw her mum half-running up the street towards her.

"Ellie, I'm so sorry. The freezer broke down. The repair man says it's too old to fix. I don't know how I'll afford a new one."

"It's all going to be okay," Jax said calmly. Since she and Beans had done the balloon magic, she felt totally confident that Mum's café was going to work out.

Her mum looked close to tears. "I don't think it *is* going to be okay. I've already spent too much money doing up the café. What if this is a mistake?"

"It's not a mistake," Jax said firmly.

But her mum wasn't listening. "What if your grandpa was right? What if I took you away from your home and friends for nothing but a selfish dream?"

Jax swallowed. Suddenly she and Mum had switched places. Just as she was starting to believe in the café, Mum had given up hope. She and Moonbeans had tried to fix things with magic, but it wasn't working.

When they got home, Jax sneaked Mum's

mobile out of her bag. "Just going to my room," she gabbled and dashed upstairs.

Beans came to greet her, stretching his back legs and yawning.

"Hello, sleepyhead," she teased. "I thought you were supposed to be on a mission?"

I just had a little afternoon nap while I was waiting for you to come home, he told her.

The little moon cat watched intently as Jax quickly punched the tiny buttons on Mum's phone. "I'm going to call Grandpa and invite him to Mum's launch," she explained. Grandpa was out, so she left a message; the same one she'd tied to her imaginary balloon.

Beans watched, blinking his amber-gold eyes. *You invited him when we did the Purr of Power.*

"I know," Jax said forlornly. "But on my planet, purring just doesn't seem to be enough."

The door opened and Mum walked in. "Have you seen my mobile?" Her eyes went wide with shock as she saw the kitten.

Beans shot under the bed, but Mum was faster. She dragged him out by his scruff.

"How long has this…this *animal* been here?" she thundered.

Jax gulped. "Mum, don't hold him like that." Her legs were shaking. She had been so sure her mum wouldn't find out. She suddenly felt as if she was trapped inside a horrible dream.

Mum realized that she was touching a real live furry kitten and hastily dropped him on the bed. "I can't *believe* you, Ellie! You watched me sneezing and wheezing, and all the time you knew what was making me ill!"

You didn't tell me I was making her sneeze. Beans seemed bewildered.

109

"You're going to take him back where he came from or I'll take him to Cat Rescue myself!" Mum yelled.

Jax burst into tears. Everything was going wrong. She was supposed to be Beans's special human. The Aunts had trusted her to help him with their mission. She didn't know how she could do that if Beans went to Cat Rescue.

There was a sudden loud buzz at the door.

"You go. I'm too angry!" her mum snapped.

Jax ran downstairs and unlocked the door with hands that had gone as shaky as her legs. A lanky young man was waiting on the step. He had spiky ginger hair and an enormous number of freckles.

Jax had to sniff back her tears. "Sorry, my mum's too busy to come to the door."

"Oh, right, only I heard you needed help doing up the café."

"We do," Jax admitted. "It's just that we haven't got much—"

But the spiky-haired young man was still earnestly explaining. "I've been trying to start up a house-painting business, but things have been really slow so I thought maybe—"

Jax shook her head. "My mum can't afford—"

"Oh, I don't want paying!" he said, to her astonishment. "I was thinking we could help each other out? Everyone knows Dolly's Diner! If I do a good job redecorating, it'll be like a free advertisement for my business. Get my name out there, kind of thing. People will see I'm not one of those cowboys, and give me more work."

Jax realized why he looked so familiar. "Are you Conrad's big brother?"

He nodded. "It was Conrad who told me your mum needed help. I meant it about the money. She can just write me a testimonial saying I'm a good worker."

"Just a sec," Jax said. She yelled up the stairs. "Mum!"

"Tell her it's Lenny," he told her.

"Lenny's come to paint the café!" Jax shouted. "He doesn't want paying!"

Mum flew downstairs. "Hi, I'm Laura Jackson," she said, beaming. "Make us all some tea, Ellie," she told Jax in a harder, colder voice than the one she'd used for Lenny.

When Jax brought the tray into the café, Mum and Lenny were chatting at one of the tables. "It's time Goose Green had a decent café," Lenny was saying. "Dolly's Diner was a dump."

Jax had arranged the leftover cupcakes on a pretty plate. She showed them to her mum. "Lilia's mum made a whole box of them. I shared the others with my class, but I saved these for you."

Her mum actually gasped. "One of the mums from your school seriously made these?" she breathed. "But they're *amazing*!" Her smile faded as suddenly as it had come. "It'll take more than cupcakes to get round me, Ellie Mae," she said sharply, and she told Lenny about the kitten.

"What's wrong with kittens?" Lenny asked with his mouth full. He'd chosen a desert island cupcake, with a marzipan palm tree.

"Mum's allergic," said Jax, swallowing.

Lenny seemed to be thinking. "Is he still here, your little cat?"

Jax nodded miserably.

"I don't think you can be allergic to him then, or I'm pretty sure you'd be sneezing your head off now," Lenny told her mum. "I don't know what you're allergic to, Mrs. Jackson—"

"Please, call me Laura," said Jax's mum.

"But I'm pretty sure it's not – what's your moggie's name?"

Jax felt a tiny spark of hope. "Beans. It's short for Moonbeans."

"You know, you're right, Lenny." Mum sounded puzzled. "I was in the same room with him. I even picked him up! And I haven't needed to use my inhaler once."

"My baby brother Troy has to be rushed to hospital if he even sees a picture of a cat!" said Lenny, draining his tea. "Right, Mrs. Jackson, what needs doing first?"

"Mum," Jax started.

Mum ignored her. "It'd be wonderful if you could wash the walls down again. I've scrubbed them twice but I'm still finding grease."

Lenny laughed. "That sounds like Dolly's. Chip fat with everything!"

"Mum," Jax tried again. This time Mum ordered her to fetch Lenny the bucket, scrubbing brush and a bottle of cleaning fluid.

Lenny unscrewed the cap from the bottle and choked. "What do they put in this stuff? Battery acid?"

"*RASHOOO!*" Mum doubled up in a humongous fit of sneezing.

Lenny grinned at Jax. "Mystery solved, I'd say."

Jax couldn't believe it! Her super-allergic mum wasn't allergic to moon cats! She was allergic to cut-price cleaning fluid!

After Jax had fetched Mum's inhaler and her mum had finally stopped sneezing, she got her chance to ask her big question. "Mum, if you're not allergic to Moonbeans, can I keep him?"

Her mum looked doubtful. She'd had a lifetime of being allergic to just about every life form on this planet. What she didn't know was that Moonbeans wasn't *from* this planet. Jax couldn't exactly explain about him being an alien, though, so she just held her breath, waiting anxiously for her mum to reach a decision.

"He is a very cute kitten," Mum admitted reluctantly. "And he's obviously a brilliant mouser! That must be why the mice moved out. Your kitty scared them off!"

That wasn't quite how it happened but Jax wasn't going to tell her mum. "Please say we can keep him, Mum? *Please!*" she begged.

Her mum's face suddenly relaxed into a smile. "Yes, Ellie Mae, you can keep him."

Jax didn't say a word. She just threw her arms round her mum. Then, feeling as light as air, she ran straight upstairs to find Beans.

"Beans, guess what! My mum's not allergic to moon cats! You can stay! *Beans?*"

She had a sudden sick feeling in her stomach. Her room felt alarmingly empty. "Beans?" she called in a shaky voice, but inside she knew. Moonbeans hadn't gone invisible. He'd just gone.

That evening, Jax and her mum searched up and down the streets of Goose Green, asking people if they'd seen a long-legged teenage

kitten with huge golden
eyes. Nobody had.

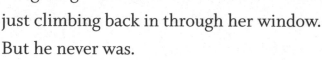

"Tomorrow I'll make
posters," Mum said,
trying to comfort her.

In the night, Jax
kept jumping awake,
imagining that Beans was
just climbing back in through her window.
But he never was.

Next morning, Jax begged Mum to let her
stay home and look for Beans, but her mum
insisted that she had to go to school.

They were just leaving the house when Jax
saw Lilia and her mum hurrying down the
street towards them. In her arms, Lilia's mum
was holding Moonbeans.

"Is this your kitty?" she asked. "He was
waiting outside our door. He kept running

ahead and looking back at us, as if he wanted us to follow."

Jax buried her face in his fur. "I thought you'd run away," she whispered.

I keep telling you, you're my human, said Moonbeans in surprise. *I thought I'd leave you and your mum to sort things out, so I went to see if Rumble had any news about my dad.*

"Has he found him?" Jax whispered into his fur.

Not yet. But he's put the word out on the street. Then I thought I'd visit Lilia and her mum.

"Why?" Jax asked softly.

Wait and see, said Moonbeans.

"Hi, it's nice to meet you finally," Lilia's mum was saying to Jax's mum. "You've taken on quite a task doing up Dolly's Diner all by yourself! I'm Nadia, by the way," she added with a warm smile. "Lilia and Jax are in the same class."

Mum gasped. "You're Lilia's mum! I've been hoping I might run into you. Did you really make those absolutely amazing cupcakes!"

"Did you like them?" Lilia's mum asked anxiously.

"I LOVED them!" said Mum. "I'd love to sell them in the café."

"*Really?*" Lilia's mum was so pleased she turned bright pink.

Beans was watching the two mums, purring his tea-kettle purr. "You *wanted* them to meet, didn't you?" Jax said softly.

Moonbeans didn't answer, he just carried on purring.

It suddenly dawned on her that this was all part of Moonbeans's mission. The Aunts had sent him to help the life forms of Goose Green live happier lives. Well, Jax and her mum were life forms, weren't they? Ever since he arrived,

120

the moon cat had been busily helping Mum
and Jax to make new friends and get their café
up and running!

But he couldn't do it without my help, she
thought.

Their mums went on chatting all the way
to school. When Jax and Lilia left them at the
gate, they were discussing what kinds of
cupcakes Lilia's mum should bake for the big
launch party.

"Has your mum got some fun ideas for the
launch?" Lilia asked.

Jax shook her head. "I'm not sure. She's been
really busy."

Lilia grinned. "That's okay, I've got loads! I'll
tell you about them at break!"

That afternoon, Mum was waiting by the
school gate. She looked happier than Jax had

seen her for ages. "Your kitten has brought us good luck!" she said, beaming.

She said people had been turning up at the café all day, leaving messages and offers of help. The lady who ran the Red Hot Wok takeaway had actually donated her old chest freezer until Mum could afford a new one. "It almost makes me believe in magic," Mum said.

Jax remembered the brightly coloured balloons floating over Goose Green, each one with its handwritten message. "Me too," she said softly.

Back at the café, Lenny was busy turning the walls sunshine-yellow. Mum sat down at one of the tables and started writing a list. Moonbeans sat at her feet, purring, looking like a proper café cat.

"There's still a lot to do before our big opening." Mum sighed.

"Me and Lilia came up with some brilliant ideas for your launch," Jax told her. "You need to get some cool flyers printed, and order helium balloons with the café's name on. Oh, and Lilia says we should have jugglers outside on the pavement."

Mum laughed. "I don't think my budget will stretch to jugglers!"

"My mate Dylan does juggling," Lenny called from his ladder. "I'll ask him if you like?"

Mum looked as if she was dreaming. "That would be wonderful."

"You still need a good name for the café," Jax reminded her.

Mum shook her head. "I've been thinking about that. Dolly's has been here so long it's like a local landmark. I'm sticking with the name everyone knows."

"At least let me give the sign a lick of paint," said Lenny.

Jax and Moonbeans watched as Lenny took down the scruffy old sign, brought it into the café and started to repaint it.

That evening, Jax had just finished eating her tea, when she noticed Beans silently heading down the stairs.

She followed him down to the café, where Lenny had left the sign to dry. "What's up?"

The Aunts say Dolly's Diner isn't the right name, said Moonbeans firmly.

Before Jax could stop him he ran across the freshly painted sign. "Are you totally *nuts*?" she gasped. Then her eyes went wide as she saw what clever Beans had done.

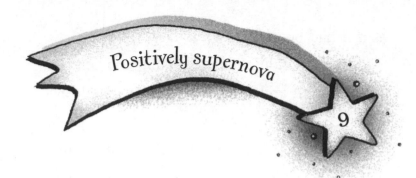

The night before the big launch, Jax and her mum stood outside the café looking up at the new sign. The light from the street lamps made the painted colours shimmer like rainbows mixed with moonlight.

"It's the perfect name," Mum said softly.

"I know," said Jax. She shot a mischievous grin at Moonbeans, who had joined them outside the café and was innocently washing a front paw. Jax had been sure Mum would ask awkward questions, but she'd just accepted the sign's magical transformation as if it had been her own idea.

Beans is totally brilliant at doing magic now, she thought, and she bent down to give him a stroke.

Mum gave a little shiver. "I'm so nervous about tomorrow, Ellie. I still haven't heard from your grandpa. I do wish he'd come."

Me too, thought Jax.

Her mum turned pale. "Suppose *no one* comes!"

"They will," Jax promised.

It wasn't just the spring sunshine streaming in through Mum's stylish new windows that made the launch party feel so special, Jax thought, as customers flocked into their café. Or the dove-grey and sunflower-yellow paint. Or even the bobbing helium balloons with the café's new name in shimmery gold letters.

It wasn't the smell of freshly
squeezed fruit juice mixing
with the aroma of cinnamon,
coffee beans and frothy hot
chocolate, or the glass-fronted

cabinets displaying Lilia's mum's delicious
cakes and pastries. It wasn't even Lenny's mate
Dylan juggling rainbow-coloured balls on the
sunny pavement outside. It was all of those
things – with an added dash of magic from
Moonbeans.

"What a marvellous atmosphere this café
has now," an old lady said to her friend. "It feels
like a big party!"

Jax wondered if she was the only human
who could see the pink shimmer that filled the
café as Beans weaved back and forth between
the customers, purring his tea-kettle purr.

Towards the end of the morning, Howard's

family came in, with Howard trailing gloomily behind them. As usual, Howard had his hair flopping over his eyes and, as usual, Jax longed to grab a pair of scissors and chop it off! "We've got cupcakes like fluffy white rabbits. They look *exactly* like your one!" Jax told him, completely forgetting that she had only seen Howard's rabbit because she was spying through Dad's telescope.

Howard looked totally spooked. "How did you know I've got a rabbit?" *Uh-oh*, thought Jax, but to her relief, Howard's little sister dragged him off to look at the cake display cabinet.

"This is the most exciting thing to happen in Goose Green for years," Howard's dad was telling Mum in a booming voice.

Jax grinned to herself. There had been some shaky moments along the way, but now Mum's café was going positively supernova!

The word made her think of Dad, which made her think of Beans's secret mission. "Has Rumble said anything about finding your dad?" she whispered to Beans.

Not yet, but he always said it would take time.

Jax looked around the crowded café. She was remembering how it looked when they moved in: dirty greasy walls; mice running around the storeroom. Without Beans's moon magic, they would never have got the café ready in time.

You did the Earth magic, Beans said, reading her mind.

"What did I do?" she asked, surprised.

You stopped Conrad being a bully. You made friends with Lilia and her mum.

Jax swallowed and finally plucked up the courage to voice a secret and terrible worry. "Now our café's open, will you go back to your world?"

Beans blinked with surprise. *Your mum's café isn't my mission. The café is just the beginning.*

Jax was so relieved, she hugged him tight. "I love you, Beans!"

She spotted her mum signalling to her across the café and felt a pang of distress. This was Mum's big day and there was still no sign of her grandpa. *He should have come*, she thought wistfully.

Mum wanted Jax and Lilia to go out into the street to hand out free cupcakes as part of the launch.

Outside the café, someone had let go of their balloon. Jax and Lilia watched it sail away over the rooftops, then they got busy handing out cupcakes. In no time, Jax only had one left: a cake with sparkly red hearts on.

"Laura's never going to make any money if she gives her cakes away for free," said a familiar grumbling voice, and Grandpa reached out to take the sparkly heart cake.

Jax gasped. "You came!"

He was just as grumpy as always, but something in his eyes told her that Grandpa was secretly delighted to see her. Was it Earth magic or moon magic that finally persuaded him to come to Mum's launch in the end? *It doesn't matter*, she thought. *He's here.*

"Daft name for a café," her grandpa grumbled. "That was your mum's idea too, I suppose?"

"It wasn't her idea actually," she said coolly.

"And I think it's a brilliant name."

"Nice colours," he admitted grudgingly. "Quite magical really."

Jax and Grandpa both stood looking up at the freshly painted sign. In rainbow-coloured letters that looked as if they'd been dipped in moonlight, it said simply: *The Dream Café*. Jax couldn't help smiling.

Thanks to Moonbeans, Dolly's Diner had been transformed into a magical meeting place where dreams came true.

And it's only just the beginning, Jax thought, remembering Moonbeans's promise. She smiled up at her grandpa. "Let's go and find Mum."

A message from Annie

Dear Readers,

Like Ellie Mae Jackson I lived just with my mum. She didn't run a café that sold magical cupcakes, she went out to work as a secretary, and in the holidays I took care of myself most days. I was often lonely and longed for a pet.

One day, most unusually, my mum took a day off from her job and even more unusually she walked me to my village school. She said she had arranged to meet one of my teachers but didn't explain why. Unlike most country people in those days, this teacher owned a car. We waited patiently outside the school gates and eventually saw him driving very carefully along the road. He stopped in front of us and I was amazed to see a tiny but extremely confident tabby kitten riding in the passenger seat. I was even more amazed when my mum explained that this kitten was for me!

I called him Tinker and he was the next best thing to a magical moon cat. He adored me from the start and, when he grew older, often tried to follow me to school. He seemed to know what time I'd be coming home and was always waiting for me on the corner. I shared all my thoughts and worries with Tinker, just like Jax does with Moonbeans, and I was absolutely convinced that he understood everything I was telling him. Like Moonbeans, Tinker often had to go out roaming on private cat business. Then, during the night he would jump in through my bedroom window, smelling of earth and wild flowers, and curl up with me until morning. I have known dozens of wonderful cats and kittens since then but none of them have been quite as magical and special as Tinker...except Beans. I hope you'll love my magical moon cat as much as I do. As a special treat, we've added a sneak preview of the next book – ENJOY!

Love and moon dust,
Annie xxx

www.anniedaltonwriter.co.uk

Calling all Magical Moon Cat Fans!

Read on for a sneak preview of Jax and Beans's next mission,

MOONBEANS AND THE SHINING STAR

But remember – it's TOP SECRET!

"Something really funny happened at school today," Jax said, twiddling a strand of her hair. "You remember Conrad? Mrs. Chaudhary sent him outside."

He wasn't bullying Lilia again? asked Beans.

Jax shook her head, remembering how she and Beans had put a stop to Conrad's bullying ways. Later, no one was sure if they really had seen the new girl turn into a flashing, sparkling, karate-kicking girl firework; but everyone agreed that Conrad was a changed boy.

"He wasn't being a bully, he was just being Conrad – you know how he gets," Jax told Beans. "Mrs. Chaudhary says he has too much energy for his own good. She told him to run twice round the playground then come back in. Conrad is so cheeky!" she said, giggling. "He ran twice around the playground, only he did it backwards! When Mrs. Chaudhary told him off, he said, 'Miss, you just said run! You never said which way!'"

Beans looked tickled. *I like Conrad.*

"He gets on with almost everybody in my class now," Jax said, then quickly corrected herself. "Everybody except Ruby-Rose. She's the one causing all the trouble nowadays."

Is Ruby-Rose the girl who has a little fluffy dog?

Moonbeans was being tactful, Jax thought

gratefully. He could have said: "Oh, Ruby-Rose
– that's the girl you secretly spied on when you
first arrived in Goose Green!" Jax had told
Beans absolutely everything that had happened
to her the day he came hurtling out of the sky
and into her life, though the part about using
her dad's telescope to spy on her neighbours
had made her hot with embarrassment. Dad
wouldn't have approved of her using his
telescope to spy on her fellow humans.

I'm a different person now, she told herself.
That was before Moonbeans came.

Aloud, she said, "Ruby-Rose just loves to
get people into trouble. No one in my class
likes her. You just have to breathe on her and
she has a hissy fit."

Did she have a hissy fit today?

"She has one *every* day," said Jax with
feeling. "The smallest thing sets her off."

What set her off today?

"Actually it was Conrad! Every time Conrad does a drawing, he has to sing. He doesn't, you know, really belt it out, he just sings under his breath. Lilia thinks he doesn't even know he's doing it. Anyway, he started singing and Ruby-Rose went bonkers! She burst into tears and went running to Mrs. Chaudhary and said he was deliberately singing the Sparkle Fluff song to make her look stupid! Miss believed her – teachers always believe Ruby-Rose. That's why she sent Conrad outside."

Beans seemed baffled. *The Sparkle Fluff song?*

Putting on a cute little-girl voice, Jax sang, "'Sparkle Fluff is full of stuff that little fairies love.' It's an advert for a pudding in a tub," she explained. "It's fluffy, like marshmallow, and it's got sparkles in – that's why it's called Sparkle

Fluff. Mum won't buy it because it's got chemicals."

Why did Ruby-Rose think Conrad was trying to make her look stupid? Beans pondered.

Jax shrugged. "Lilia said that Ruby-Rose did the voice for the little cartoon fairy in the commercial. She does all these drama classes after school." She gave Beans a mischievous grin. "That's probably why she's so good at fooling teachers."

Jax didn't want to think about Ruby-Rose for a minute more than she had to. She jumped off the bed with a bounce. "Is that my three interesting things?"

Yes, thank you, said Beans politely.

"Good, because I'm starving! I'm going to beg Mum for a triple-chocolate cupcake. Coming?"

Beans followed her as far as the downstairs

hall then he suddenly stopped. *There's someone I need to see,* he said.

Jax was disappointed. She had just assumed they'd spend the rest of the day together. *Get used to it, Jax,* she told herself. *He's a moon cat on a mission. Not a cuddly little pet.*

She wondered if he was going to see Rumble, the battle-scarred old tomcat Beans hung around with sometimes. Not even the Aunts knew this, but Beans had another personal reason for wanting to visit Earth: he had always longed to meet his dad. And the old street cat had promised to use his contacts to help track him down.

"Will you be back before I go to bed?" Jax asked him hopefully.

Beans had stopped listening. He was gingerly approaching the cat flap. He could have used magic to get out of the house, but Jax and Beans wanted their neighbours to believe that he was a normal kitten. Unfortunately Beans *really* hated his cat flap and treated it like a cunning beast with snapping jaws that had to be outwitted. As he preferred to fight his cat-flap battles in private, Jax tactfully left him to it.

As she tiptoed away, she heard him hurl himself violently at the door. There was a lot of desperate scrabbling, followed by a shattering *THWACK!* as he finally disappeared.

Poor Beans, she thought, giggling. She was still smirking as she slipped through the side door into the café. Then she suddenly stopped in her tracks. Was it her imagination, or was their café looking unusually *shimmery*?

When her mum started renovating Dolly's Diner, some local people had complained. They thought Mum was going to turn it into some snobby upscale café. They wanted to keep

Dolly's the way it was, chip fat and all. Then Moonbeans came, and suddenly everyone started offering to help. Conrad's big brother Lenny came to finish the decorating. Mei Lee from the Red Hot Wok donated her spare freezer. Lilia's mum Nadia turned out to be a total genius at making cupcakes and cookies. If Jax hadn't known better, she might have thought all those things just happened by chance… After the café opened, Mum's customers constantly commented on its friendly vibe. They saw Moonbeans strolling and purring between the tables but they didn't make a connection. They thought they just kept coming back because Jax's mum served good coffee and cakes. Only Jax and Beans knew the truth.

The Aunts had a daring and ambitious plan for Planet Earth and they had chosen

Moonbeans and Jax to put it into action right here in Goose Green. Jax still had no clue which local human the Aunts would ask them to help next, but she knew it would be someone who came into Mum's café. Moonbeans had explained that the Dream Café was a crucial part of the Aunts' plan.

The thought made her heart beat faster. Anyone could walk into a café. A princess could walk into a café. Someone could burst in begging them to hide her from kidnappers. Whoever it was, it would be someone in real trouble, the kind of trouble that only a nine-year-old girl with a magical moon cat could fix.

Is it you? Jax asked each of the customers silently.

She wasn't imagining the glimmer, the café seemed to be getting more shimmery by the minute…and were those *pink sparkles* falling softly through the air?

It's happening! The mission is starting. Jax hugged herself with excitement. She noticed her mum hurrying over to greet two new customers who had just walked in. And the pink sparkles faded like a dream as she recognized the scowling face of Ruby-Rose…

Is helping stuck-up Ruby-Rose REALLY Jax and Beans's next mission?

Find out what happens next in

* Moonbeans *
and the Shining Star

Deliciously delectable recipes from
THE DREAM CAFÉ

Bring a little moon-cat magic into your life by making your own gorgeous cupcakes. Yum!

Moonbeans's magic cupcakes

FOR THE CUPCAKES (makes 12)

You will need:

175g (6oz) self-raising flour

175g (6oz) soft margarine

175g (6oz) caster sugar

1 teaspoon of vanilla essence

3 medium eggs

A 12-hole deep muffin tray and 12 paper muffin cases

1. Heat the oven to 180°C / Gas mark 4. Put a paper muffin case in each hole in the tray.

2. Sift the flour into a large mixing bowl. Add the margarine, sugar and vanilla essence.

3. Break the eggs into a cup, then pour them into the bowl. Stir until you have a smooth mixture.

4. Spoon the mixture into the paper cases, dividing it evenly between them.

5. Bake for 20-25 minutes or until firm and golden on top.

6. Leave the cooked cakes in the tray for a few minutes. Then put them on a wire rack to cool. Meanwhile, make the buttercream.

For the buttercream

No cupcake is truly finished until it's decorated with yummy buttercream. Here are Jax's fave magical mixtures.

COOL CLASSIC BUTTERCREAM

You will need:

100g (4oz) softened, unsalted butter/soft margarine

225g (8oz) icing sugar

1 tablespoon of milk

½ teaspoon of vanilla essence

1. Put the butter or margarine in a large mixing bowl and beat with a wooden spoon until it becomes soft and fluffy.

2. Sift one third of the icing sugar into the bowl and stir it in. Then, sift the rest of the icing sugar over the mixture.

3. Add the milk and vanilla. Beat quickly, until you have a pale and fluffy mixture.

CHOCOLATE TREAT

Just use 175g (6oz) of icing sugar and sift in 40g (1½oz) of cocoa powder instead for a chocolate topping.

ZINGY CITRUS

Swap the milk and vanilla with the finely grated rind from 1 orange, 1 lemon or 2 limes, and 2 teaspoons of juice from the fruit, for a zingy citrus flavour.

*Add a couple of drops of food colouring for pretty pastel or bright and bold decorations.

*Decorate your cupcakes with mini-sweets or sugar sprinkles for extra sparkle.

Cherry chocolate brownies

These scrumptious brownies have a crispy top and
a squidgy middle, dotted with nuts and cherries.
Jax loves to eat her brownies warm with ice-cream
and chocolate sauce. If, like Grandpa, you prefer
more traditional brownies, just leave out
the cherries.

(Makes 12-16)

You will need:

100g (4oz) plain chocolate

2 large eggs

125g (4½oz) softened butter or soft margarine

275g (10oz) caster sugar

½ teaspoon of vanilla essence

50g (2oz) self-raising flour

25g (1oz) plain flour

2 tablespoons of cocoa powder

100g (4oz) dried cherries

100g (4oz) walnut or pecan pieces (optional)

A 20cm (8in) square cake tin

1. Heat the oven to 180°C / Gas mark 4. Grease and line the cake tin.

2. Melt the chocolate. To do this, put the chocolate in a heatproof bowl. Fill a pan a quarter full of water and put it over a medium heat. Then carefully lower the bowl into the pan. Leave for 5 minutes, then stir the chocolate until it is melted.

3. Break the eggs into a small bowl. Beat them with a fork.

4. Put the butter or margarine, sugar and vanilla in a big bowl. Beat until they are fluffy. Add the eggs a little at a time, beating well.

5. Sift both types of flour and the cocoa powder into the bowl. Add the melted chocolate. Mix well.

6. Mix in the cherries and nuts. Scrape the mixture into the tin. Smooth the top with the back of a spoon.

7. Bake for 35 minutes, until slightly risen. It should have a crust on top but a soft middle.

8. Leave in the tin for 20 minutes to cool. Cut into 12-16 pieces.

Fancy some chocolate sauce?

* You will need 100g (4oz) chocolate drops, 2 tablespoons of golden syrup or honey and 1 tablespoon of water.

* Put all the ingredients in a pan over a low heat. Stir until you have a glossy mixture. Leave to cool for a few minutes before eating. Deee-li-cious!

🌸 Orange Drizzle Cupcakes

These moist, tangy cupcakes are made using cornmeal (polenta) instead of flour, which means they are wheat and gluten-free. You can even make them dairy-free by using dairy-free spread instead of butter.

(Makes 12)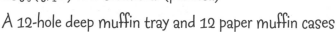

You will need:

3 oranges

175g (6oz) softened butter or soft margarine

175g (6oz) caster sugar

3 medium eggs

1½ teaspoons of gluten-free baking powder

165g (5½oz) fine cornmeal (polenta)

A 12-hole deep muffin tray and 12 paper muffin cases

FOR THE ORANGE GLACÉ ICING

You will need:

175g (6oz) icing sugar

1. Heat the oven to 190°C / Gas mark 5. Put a paper case in each hollow of the muffin tray.

2. Grate the zest from the oranges. Put it in a big bowl.

3. Squeeze the juice from the oranges. Put 1½ tablespoons of juice in a bowl for the glacé icing and the rest in a jug.

4. Put the butter or margarine and caster sugar in the bowl with the zest. Beat until the mixture is pale and fluffy.

5. Break an egg into a small bowl. Beat it with a fork. Tip it into the big bowl and mix it in. Do the same with the other eggs.

6. Put the baking powder and cornmeal in the bowl. Add one tablespoon of orange juice from the jug. Mix gently.

7. Spoon the mixture into the paper cases. Bake for 20 minutes until golden and firm.

8. Carefully pour the juice from the jug over the hot cakes. Leave them in the tin to cool.

9. To make the orange glacé icing, sift the icing sugar into a bowl. Mix in the juice you put in the bowl earlier. The icing should be quite runny for drizzling.

10. Scoop up some icing. Hold the spoon over a cake. Tip the spoon, then move it over the cake, leaving a trail of icing.

If you loved these cupcakes, why not get creative and add a dash of something different:

FOR LEMON OR LIME DRIZZLE CUPCAKES

Replace the oranges with 3 lemons or 6 limes.

FOR CHOCOLATE ORANGE CUPCAKES

At step 5, use just 125g (4½oz) cornmeal and sift 40g (1½oz) cocoa powder into the bowl too. Instead of the icing, melt 100g (4oz) chocolate and drizzle it over the top.

For top tips on decorating your delicious cakes and fab bonus colouring pages, log on to www.magicalmooncat.com

You can find all these **YUMMY** recipes,
plus **LOADS** more in

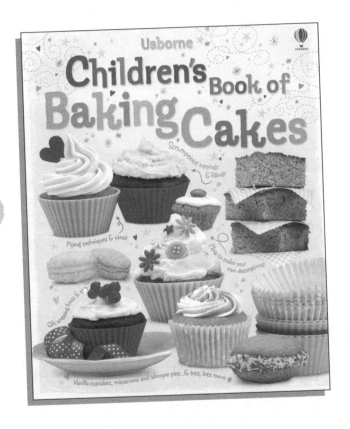

My Magical Moon Cat Page

Hi everyone, it's me, Jax. I hope the story of my magical moon cat and our Dream Café has inspired you to get creative.

Use this page to keep a note of your TOP SECRET missions.

Make it sparkle with your own space-tastic stickers!

Jot down your fave recipes here.

Decorate it with your own Moonbeans doodles.

Magical Moon Cat

Join Jax and Moonbeans and collect every magical mission!

Moonbeans and the Shining Star

When Moonbeans announces he's on a mission to cheer up stroppy starlet, Ruby-Rose, Jax is dismayed. Ruby-Rose thinks she's the bee's knees because she goes to stage school. But is it just an act?

ISBN: 9781409526322

Moonbeans and the Talent Show

Hubble, the white rabbit, is worried about his owner, Howard. He dreams of performing a dazzling magic act in the school talent show, but his act has more mishaps than magic. Can Jax and Beans help Howard shine?

ISBN: 9781409526339

Moonbeans and the Circus of Wishes

Beans's wish to find his Earth-cat dad looks set to come true, after Jax and Beans discover he's living with a travelling circus. But Jax is worried. Could this spell the end of her adventures with her magical moon cat?

ISBN: 9781409526346

For more amazing adventures,
zoom to www.fiction.usborne.com